Snowflake

Florrie was busy pulling out all the sparkly things from the busy box.

"Look, Pom," she said, "tinsel!
What shall I make today?"

But Baby Pom ran off without answering. She was busy getting the Fimbling Feeling.

"I can feel a twinkling,
I can hear a sound,
It's telling me there's something
Waiting to be found!
Where is it? Where is it?
What could it be?
I think it might be over there.
Let's go and see!"

Baby Pom looked up and saw something spinning

down,

down,

down,

towards her.

"Oooh," she said, putting out her hand to catch it. "Shiny! Sparkly! Pom catch it!"

Just then, Fimbo came along.

"What have you caught?" he asked.

But when Baby Pom opened her hand, the shiny, sparkly thing had gone.

"It's all gone," she said, then, "Oh, pretty!" as she caught another one.

Baby Pom ran off to show Florrie.

"Florrie, Florrie, Florrie!" she called. "Pom a Fimbly Find!"

"What have you found?" asked Florrie.

Baby Pom opened her hand but the shiny, sparkly thing had gone.

"Hello, my lovelies," said Bessie, landing nearby. "You caught a snowflake, and it melted in your warm hand. That's why it's gone."

"Oh," said Baby Pom, feeling sad.

But when the snow began to fall again, Baby Pom and Florrie made up a song and dance about snowflakes.

When the snow stopped falling, Baby Pom felt sad again.

"Shall we make snowflakes that don't melt away?" asked Florrie.

"Pom like," said Baby Pom.

So Florrie folded and tore a piece of paper, and when she opened it up, there was a snowflake. Baby Pom made snowflakes by tearing her paper into tiny pieces.

Rockit was sitting by the Bubble Fall watching a snowflake spin down, down, down, until it landed on the end of his nose.

"Glung! Ohh, that tickles," giggled Rockit.

And when Roly Mo pushed his nose out of the ground, a snowflake landed right on the end of it.

"Snow!" chuckled Roly Mo.

"Hooray!" called Rockit, who felt so happy that he boing, boing, boing, boinged! right to the top of the Bubble Fall, where he did a snowflake song and dance.

The Fimbles were busy singing and dancing along when they met Rockit.

And just as Florrie showed them the paper snowflake… it stopped snowing.

"All gone," said Baby Pom.

But when she looked up into the sky, a shiny, sparkly snowflake came spinning down, down, down, and it landed on the end of her nose. Baby Pom giggled, and everyone sang the snowflake song over and over again.